This book belongs to
my friend:

_____

A NOTE TO PARENTS

In *Blue's Backyard Mystery*, Blue and her friends discover that their strawberries are missing. Who took them? Read along, and see if you and your child can solve the mystery before the Backyard Detectives do.

Involve your child in the story by discussing all of the clues presented. For instance, ask her which animal has footprints like the ones in the story, or if she thinks ants could have taken the strawberries so quickly. By using both visual and textual clues, your child will learn to pay attention to details and build deductive reasoning skills. Before reading the book's conclusion, encourage your child to guess who or what is the culprit.

After solving the mystery, head outside to explore nature on your own. Find some ways animals and insects use problem-solving skills. For example, what do squirrels do to prepare for winter? Or, what materials do birds use to make nests? Enjoy the outdoors! Prepare a picnic (including strawberries!); find pictures in the clouds; watch bees pollinate flowers or a spider spin a web. By spending quality time outside as often as possible, you will be teaching your child to appreciate nature.

Learning Fundamental: **problem solving**

For more parent and kid-friendly activities, go to www.nickjr.com.

Blue's Backyard Mystery

Published by Scholastic Inc., 90 Old Sherman Turnpike, Danbury, CT 06816

SCHOLASTIC and associated logos are trademarks and/or registered trademarks of Scholastic Inc.

ISBN 0-7172-6631-1

Printed in the U.S.A.

First Scholastic Printing, April 2003

Blue's Backyard Mystery

by
Tod Olson

illustrated by
Victoria Miller

SCHOLASTIC INC.

New York   Toronto   London   Auckland   Sydney
Mexico City   New Delhi   Hong Kong   Buenos Aires

One beautiful day, Blue and her friends Magenta and
Periwinkle were enjoying a picnic in Blue's backyard.

They had the whole afternoon ahead of them.

"Hey, I have an idea. Let's play the Cloud Game!"
Blue suggested.

They all lay on their backs and looked up at the sky.

"I see a boat," said Blue.
"I see a dinosaur," said Magenta.

"I see a banana!" Periwinkle giggled.

Then Periwinkle decided that all this cloud watching was making him hungry again. So he said, "Let's get back to our peri-perfect picnic."

That's when they noticed something was missing!

"Hey, the strawberries are gone!" Periwinkle exclaimed.

"Where could they be?" asked Magenta.
"Look," Blue shouted, "footprints!"

Blue jumped up. "I know what we can do!" She ran into the house and returned with a magnifying glass. "Let's follow the tracks," she suggested.

"Good idea!" said Periwinkle. "I bet they'll lead us to the strawberries."

"We'll be the Backyard Detectives," Magenta said excitedly.

So the Backyard Detectives set off through the
beautiful day in search of the missing strawberries.

Suddenly Blue stopped short. Then she giggled.
"I thought I saw a strawberry," she told her friends.

"It's a flower," said Magenta. "Wow!
Look at all the dandelions!"
Periwinkle smiled. "I have an idea."

Periwinkle wove a string of dandelions into a crown. Magenta made a necklace. "What are you going to make, Blue?" they asked.

Blue thought for a moment. "I know! I'll make a Backyard Detective badge."

After Blue finished, Periwinkle said, "Lead the way, Detective Blue!"

"Hey, guys," Blue exclaimed, "somebody dropped a piece of strawberry!"

"And look who found it," said Magenta, peering through the magnifying glass.

"Wow, cool!" exclaimed Periwinkle. "Ants!"

"They're carrying seeds, too," Blue said. "Maybe whoever took the strawberries likes seeds."

So the Backyard Detectives set off through the beautiful day in search of the missing strawberries.

Along the way they found ladybugs. "Their footprints don't look like the ones we're following," Magenta said.

They found frogs. "They don't eat seeds Blue said.

And they found a praying mantis. "I don't think he can carry a strawberry," Periwinkle said.

The tracks crossed the sandtable.

"Want to play?" Pail asked.

"Sorry, we can't," Blue explained. "We're searching for missing strawberries."

"I saw who took the strawberries," Shovel squealed. "I'll give you a hint." He drew a picture in the sand.

"An acorn," Magenta said thoughtfully. "Oh, I know who it might be!"

So the Backyard Detectives set off through the beautiful day in search of the missing strawberries.

Suddenly they spotted a second set of tracks. Periwinkle peered through the magnifying glass. "Hmm," he wondered, "could these lead us to the strawberries?"

"I don't know," Blue replied. "They look different from the other footprints."

"I see why," Magenta laughed.

"Hi, Tickety!" Periwinkle called. "Have you seen who took our missing strawberries?"

Tickety shook her head. "But I think you're getting close," she said, pointing to another piece of strawberry on the ground.

"It looks like someone was getting hungry,"
Blue said.

So the Backyard Detectives set off through the
beautiful day in search of the missing strawberries.

"The tracks end here," Blue said, standing at the base of a big tree.

"But who took the strawberries?" Magenta asked.

The Backyard Detectives looked left . . . then they looked right . . .

. . . and finally they looked up.

"Well," said Blue, "we found our answer!"

The Backyard Detectives all laughed.

Then they set off through the beautiful day in search of another mystery.